The Wonder of Easter

by Matt Mitter

illustrated by Samuel J. Butcher

A GOLDEN BOOK • NEW YORK

Easter is a special time,
A joyful holiday,

A time to join with family
To worship and to pray.

Easter comes with baskets
And with Easter eggs galore,

And Easter cards—the handmade kind—
That moms and dads adore!

Easter brings a new spring dress
With lace and ribbons on it,

And fancy hats with frills to match,
Or, if you like, a bonnet.

At Easter time we see new life
Beginning to appear.

Babies, too, of every kind
Arrive this time each year. . . .

Fluffy, yellow, chirping chicks
Come popping out of eggs,

And woolly lambs come tottering
On thin, unsteady legs.

As spring's fresh breezes chase away
The winter's ice and snow,

Heaven's gentle showers help
The Easter flowers grow.

The wet world welcomes spring's
   soft showers,
And once the clouds drip-dry,

The sun paints brilliant rainbows
'Cross a soft blue Easter sky.

The warmer weather coaxes us
To come and play outside—

To skip or skate or swim or swing
Or take a scooter ride!

Easter is a time to share
With those we love to see—

To tiptoe through the tulips
For a friendly cup of tea.

Just as we sow seeds to help
Our gardens sprout anew,

It seems that Heaven sows our world
With love at Easter, too.

God's love blooms in hearts again,
As flowers do each spring,

And we reach out with tenderness
To every living thing.

At Easter let us celebrate
The wonders of our Earth,
And thank God for the gift of life
And promise of rebirth.